THERE'S A HIPPOPOTAMUS ON OUR ROOF EATING CAKE

HODDER AND STOUGHTON

SYDNEY AUCKLAND LONDON TORONTO

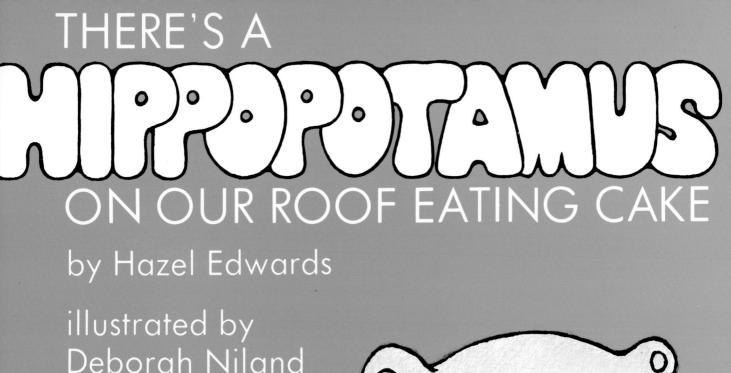

THERE'S A
HIPPOPOTAMUS
ON OUR ROOF EATING CAKE

by Hazel Edwards

illustrated by
Deborah Niland

First published in 1980 by
Hodder and Stoughton (Australia) Pty Limited
2 Apollo Place, Lane Cove NSW 2066

**This edition first published 1982,
Reprinted 1982, 1983, 1984 (twice), 1985**

National Library of Australia
card number and ISBN
0 340 28697 0

Typeset by Savage & Co. Pty Ltd, Brisbane, Queensland
Printed in Hong Kong

Our roof leaks.
Drip!
Drip!
Drip!

My Daddy says there's a hole in our roof.
I know why there's a hole.
There's a hippopotamus on our roof eating cake.

He can do what he likes.
Drip!
Drip!
Drip!
My hippopotamus doesn't like baths.
He's having a shower.
I know, because I heard him.
There's a hippopotamus on our roof having a shower.

Mummy is on a diet.
She eats lettuce, tomato and cheese.
My big brother eats peanut butter sandwiches.
I eat honey sandwiches.
The hippopotamus on our roof eats cake all the time.

Mummy asked about the cake. "Is it birthday cake?"
"No."
"Is it chocolate cake?"
"No."
"Is it special cake?"
"Yes!"
There's a hippopotamus on our roof eating special cake.

Yesterday I fell over and cut my knee.
It hurt.
There was a lot of blood.
At the hospital, the doctor put three stitches in my knee.
I cried.

Last night, the hippopotamus told me something.
He's got a sore knee too.
There's a hippopotamus on our roof
     with a bandage on his knee.

There's a hippopotamus on our roof watching television.
He is very big.
He can do what he likes.
Mummy won't let me watch television.
After dinner and a story I have to go to bed.
My hippopotamus watches.
I know he does.
There's a hippopotamus on our roof watching television.

Today I was naughty.
I drew on Daddy's best book.
Daddy gave me a smack.
Down here, no one is my friend.
My hippopotamus lives on the roof.
He's my friend.
I know.

He isn't cross.
No one smacks him.
He's too big.
He can draw anything.
There's a hippopotamus on our roof
    drawing with crayons.

He wasn't there last night.
I know why.
He told me.
He went to work.

My hippopotamus works part-time at the zoo.
Zoo visitors look at animals.
At the zoo, he watches people.
When he's not working,
my hippopotamus eats cake on our roof.

There's a hippopotamus on our roof riding a bike.
I've got a bike.
Mummy won't let me ride on the road.
There are cars on the road.
There are no cars on the roof.
He can ride anywhere.
I know he can.
There's a hippopotamus on our roof riding a bike.

The men fixed the roof today.
Bang, bang, bang! No more drips.
They didn't see my hippopotamus.
He climbed down the ladder while the men had lunch.
He'll be back tonight.
Then I can say —

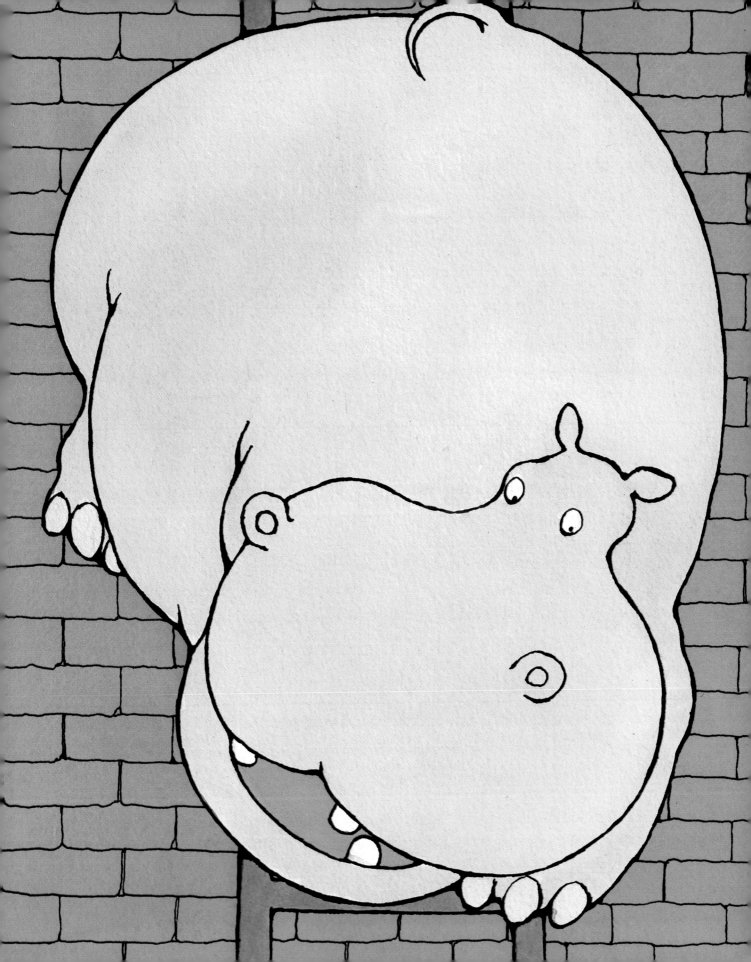

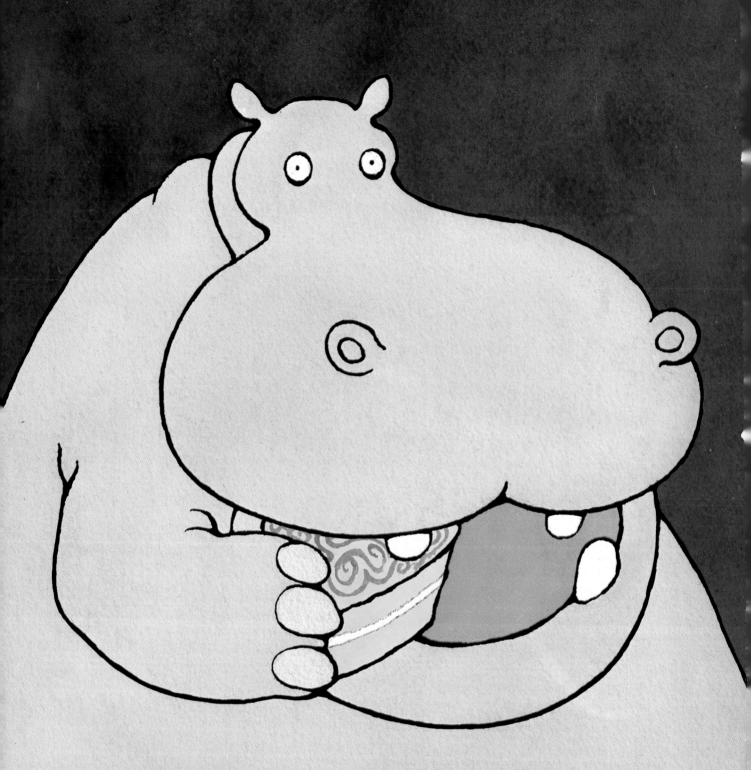

"There's a hippopotamus on our roof eating cake."

What the Ladybird Heard

For New End Primary School ~ JD

For Noah and Eva ~ LM

First published 2009 by Macmillan Children's Books
This edition published 2021 by Macmillan Children's Books
an imprint of Pan Macmillan
The Smithson, 6 Briset Street, London EC1M 5NR
Associated companies throughout the world.
www.panmacmillan.com

ISBN: 978-1-5290-5140-7

1 3 5 7 9 8 6 4 2

A CIP catalogue record for this book is available from the British Library.

Printed in China.

What the Ladybird Heard

JULIA DONALDSON ★ LYDIA MONKS

MACMILLAN CHILDREN'S BOOKS

Once upon a farm lived a fat red hen,
A duck in a pond and a goose in a pen,
A woolly sheep, a hairy hog,
A handsome horse and a dainty dog,
A cat that miaowed and a cat that purred,

A fine prize cow . . .
and a ladybird.

And the cow said, "MOO!"

and the hen said, "CLUCK!"

"HISS!" said the goose

and "QUACK!" said the duck.

"NEIGH!" said the horse.

"OINK!" said the hog.

"BAA!" said the sheep

and "WOOF!" said the dog.

One cat miaowed while the other one purred ...

And the ladybird said never a word.

But the ladybird saw,
And the ladybird heard . . .

She saw two men in a big black van,
With a map and a key and a cunning plan.
And she heard them whisper, "This is how
We're going to steal the fine prize cow:

"Open the gate at dead of night.
Pass the horse and then turn right.
Round the duck pond, past the hog
(Be careful not to wake the dog).
Left past the sheep, then straight ahead
And in through the door of the prize cow's shed!"

And the little spotty ladybird
(Who never before had said a word)
Told the animals, "This is how
Two thieves are planning to steal the cow:
They'll open the gate at dead of night.
Pass the horse and then turn right.

Round the duck pond, past the hog
(Being careful not to wake the dog).
Left past the sheep, then straight ahead
And in through the door of the prize cow's shed!"

"NEIGH!" said the horse.

"OINK!" said the hog.

"BAA!" said the sheep. "WOOF!" said the dog.

And both the cats began to miaow:
"We can't let them steal the fine prize cow!"

But the ladybird had a good idea
And she whispered it into each animal ear.

At dead of night the two bad men
(Hefty Hugh and Lanky Len)
Opened the gate while the farmer slept
And tiptoe into the farm they crept.

Then the goose said, "NEIGH!" with all her might.
And Len said, "That's the horse – turn right."

NEIGH!

And the dainty dog began to QUACK.
"The duck!" said Hugh.
"We're right on track."

QUACK!

OINK! OINK!

OINK!

"OINK," said the cats.
"There goes the hog!
Be careful not to wake the dog."

"BAA BAA BAA," said the fat red hen.
"The sheep! We're nearly there," said Len.

Then the duck on the pond said, "MOO MOO MOO!"
"Two more steps to go!" said Hugh.

BAA!

MOO!

And they both stepped into the duck pond —

SPLOSH!

And the farmer woke and said, "Golly gosh!"
And he called the cops, and they came — NEE NAH!
And they threw the thieves in their panda car.

Then the cow said, "MOO!"

and the hen said, "CLUCK!"

"HISS!" said the goose
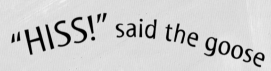

and "QUACK!" said the duck.